The Message, the Promise, and How Pigs Figure In

by M. J. Cosson

Cover Illustration: Sue F. Cornelison
Inside Illustration: Sue F. Cornelison

Text © 2001 by Perfection Learning® Corporation.

All rights reserved. No part of this book may be used or reproduced in
any manner whatsoever without written permission from the publisher.
Printed in the United States of America. For information, contact

Perfection Learning® Corporation

1000 North Second Avenue, P.O. Box 500

Logan, Iowa 51546-0500.

Phone: 1-800-831-4190 • Fax: 1-712-644-2392

Paperback ISBN 0-7891-5351-3

Cover Craft® ISBN 0-7807-9729-9

Printed in the U.S.A.

2 3 4 5 6 7 PP 10 09 08 07 06 05

Table of Contents

WE'RE DROWNING IN PIG POOP
Planet
Bacon
PIGS NEED SPACE
SUPER SWINE

1

Me

Something strange happened to me. It started a whole chain of events. It happened when I was scuba diving in Maui. I made a promise to a fish. And it changed my life.

Part of my therapy was to write about it. Well, it wasn't really therapy. But it was a suggestion from my shrink.

I agreed that it was a good idea to write about it. I wanted to remember it just as it had happened. I also decided that it was time I came out with it.

People think I'm driven. I am. And the promise is what's driving me.

The whole thing began with my parents' divorce. I'm an only child.

My mom's a pediatrician. I think that has something to do with why there's just me. My mom sees kids all day long. And she sees them at their worst. Who'd want to come home to more of that?

My dad's an anesthesiologist. He puts people under and checks on them during surgery. He's very precise. He knows the human body and how it reacts to things.

Anyway, Mom and Dad hadn't said much to each other for a long time. I guess the divorce was in the cards.

After the divorce, they both started paying more attention to me. Mom changed her work schedule so she could be home to fix dinner. Dad started planning things we could do together. All this when I'd rather be somewhere else—with someone else.

Dad got this idea to take scuba diving lessons. He signed us up at a dive shop. For a month, we spent every Saturday in a swimming pool.

They made us do things you wouldn't believe. One thing we had to do was jump in with all our gear in our hands, including our air tanks. Then we had to stay underwater while we put it all on.

The whole course was a lot of work. There was a written test too. That was fine for Dad. All he had to do was go to work. But I had school *and* homework too. Anyway, we both passed.

As a reward for passing the course, Dad decided we'd go diving in Maui. I thought that was kind of weird because that's where he and Mom went on their honeymoon. Maybe Dad thought that if he went back to where it all began, everything could be laid to rest neatly. That's the kind of guy he is. Like I said, he's very precise.

So last summer, Dad and I went to Maui. It's one of the Hawaiian Islands. It has mountains, volcanoes, tropical areas, and some neat towns. And, of course, there were the babes in bikinis.

Dad and I really had a good time looking at the scenery. It was a real bonding experience.

I guess I need to tell you who the "me" is who's writing this. My name is Jonathan Matthew Olivera. I'm 14. And I'm in eighth grade at Hudson Middle School in Saratoga, Illinois.

I run track and belong to the Environmental Action Club. In fact, I'm co-president of the club this year. I had to be after I made the promise.

I'm also trying to start a scuba diving club. But not too many kids in Saratoga dive. There's no place to do it unless you want to dive in a rock quarry or a farm pond. I don't advise either—especially the pond.

I brag a lot. Maybe because I'm a Leo. Or maybe because I'm an only child. I know I do it. And I know I shouldn't. But I can't seem to help it. I have a large voice and it just booms out.

I'm smart too. Oops—there I go again. I just can't seem to stop bragging.

Mom is Anglo with blond hair and blue eyes. Dad's Latino. That makes me Anglo Latino.

I have blond hair and brown eyes. I know the sun's bad for my skin, but I love it anyway. In the summer, I have a great tan. And my hair gets all bleached out.

I have to admit that I like my looks—except for my height. I'm only 5' 4". I wish I were taller. But I try not to let it bother me. Tom Cruise is short and it hasn't hurt him.

2

The Crater

Okay, that's enough about me. Here's the real story.

It was a beautiful, sunny Maui morning. The mist was clearing and the aqua water was calm. The air and water were both about 80 degrees.

My dad and I carried our scuba gear down the dock. We stopped at Captain Andy's Dive Boat.

Captain Andy was a crusty old guy. He had a red face and a grizzled red beard. He shouted, "Aloha, divers! Welcome aboard!"

There were six divers on board. That meant everyone would have a dive buddy. A dive buddy was someone who kept a close watch on you. And you kept a close watch on him.

I was the only kid there. Besides Captain Andy, there was Aaron, the divemaster. Aaron was Captain Andy's younger brother. He looked just like him.

During the dives, Captain Andy would stay on the boat. Aaron would lead the group underwater.

Captain Andy pointed out the snacks and drinks, the emergency equipment, the air tanks, and some books about marine life. He showed us how to flush the head (the toilet). Then he started the engine and barked directions over its roar.

"It will take about 20 minutes to get to Molokini Crater," he shouted. "Has anybody been there before?"

No one had. Captain Andy continued loudly, "It's a beautiful place. It's an extinct, submerged volcano dome with part of the rim above water. See that crescent shape out there?" We all looked and nodded.

"That's it. We'll dive on the inside of the crater first. Later, snorkelers and glass-bottom boats will take over the crater. Then we'll dive along the back wall where it's less crowded."

"The inside of the crater is fairly shallow. But at the back wall, it's 350 feet to the ocean floor."

Dad broke in, "We're not diving that deep, are we? My son and I are only certified to go 100 feet."

"Our first dive will be inside the crater. You'll go down and across the floor. We'll go 70 feet deep. Then we'll have a rest period. Our last dive will be a drift dive at the back wall. We'll only go 50 feet deep."

Dad nodded and looked at me. I knew that look only too well. It meant "follow directions and obey orders."

I'd seen that look all my life. I didn't mean that in a bad way. It was just a fact. I supposed when I was a dad, I'd probably be the same way. But it was a little hard to imagine at the time.

Dad had told me that Molokini was a vent from Haleakala. Haleakala was the big mountain volcano on Maui. We'd already visited it.

The volcano was a group of huge mounds. The mounds changed color as the sun and clouds shifted across the sky. Then the volcano looked like another planet.

We got closer to Molokini. I had this weird feeling that the crater could still blow. That made the dive more exciting than ever.

3

First Dive

The boat anchored at the tip of the crescent. We put on our gear—wet suits, weight belts, boots, masks, tanks, dive watches, dive computers, and fins.

We each pulled on a buoyancy compensator (bc). That's a vest that we can fill with air and use as a life jacket.

We checked our regulators. They're the mouthpieces and hoses that scuba divers breathe through. They were attached to the air tanks.

Dad also had an underwater camera strapped to his arm. He wanted to catch all of our action on film.

Then we shuffled to the back of the boat. When we got all that stuff on, we were carrying around a lot of weight. One by one, we took a giant stride into the ocean.

Once we got into the water, we gained a little grace. We deflated our bcs and swam down about 20 feet.

The water was so clear. We could see a long way off. The bright sunlight filtered through the blue water. It made everything look magical.

Aaron led us down toward the crater floor. The bright coral was just background for the fish. They were the real stars.

The fish were decked out in bright blue, yellow, pink, and green. Even the black and white on them glowed. There was something about the light in the water. It just couldn't be captured on film. But Dad gave it his best shot.

We all followed Aaron across the crater's floor. He stopped now and then to point to a fish or other sea creature.

Aaron had told us to signal when our air got to 700 psi (pounds per square inch). We'd each started out with 3,000 psi. We were supposed to stay down for 35 minutes. But if anybody got to 700 psi before the time was up, the whole group would have to surface.

We swam along, listening to our own breathing. It was all we could hear. Inhale, exhale. Inhale, exhale.

We swam above a moray eel in search of food. It had a mean-looking face but a classy body. It was velvet black with small white dots.

Aaron picked up a cucumber-shaped object about a foot long. Some rose-colored stuff squirted out the end. He laid it back on the ocean floor. We swam on.

A large, pearl-colored fish swam along like it was one of our group. I swear it was watching me. It even seemed to be following me.

I made eye contact with the fish. And if I swam behind or ahead, it would tip its eye to maintain contact.

It was flat, oval-shaped, and almost two feet long. It had a large head and electric blue eyes. Its pearly scales ran from pink to purple to blue as the light played on them.

All of the fish amazed me. They were watching us as much as we were watching them. Most swam away from us, though.

But this pearl-colored fish stayed right by my side. I wondered if it was waiting for a handout.

All of a sudden, I was surrounded by a school of

bright yellow butterfly fish. Dad was right there with the camera.

By this point, we'd come full circle. We were back at the dive boat. Aaron motioned that it was time to go up.

The pearl fish was still tagging along. It watched me float up to the boat.

Since we were deep in the water, there was a lot more pressure on our bodies. Weird things were happening inside us. So we had to go up slowly to give things a chance to get back to normal. It's called *outgassing*.

We went up more slowly than our breath bubbles. We knew we probably wouldn't get the bends as long as our bubbles went up faster than we did. To be safe, we made a two-minute safety stop about 15 feet from the surface. We just hung there in the water, looking at our watches.

After the hang, we popped to the surface and swam to the boat. Captain Andy took our fins and helped us on board. We were all so excited that we started jabbering like little kids.

"Did you see how long that moray was?"

"Scary! Did you see its fangs?"

"What was that thing you picked up, Aaron?"

"It was a sea cucumber."

"Did you see the humuhumu-nukunuku-apua'a?"

"The *what*?"

"The fish with the yellow marks and blue fins. It's also called a *Picasso triggerfish*."

"Yeah. It's the state fish of Hawaii. It looks like a Picasso painting."

We peeled out of our wet suits. We let the sun warm us. Boy, did that feel fine. I couldn't believe I was having such a great time with grown-ups.

4

Wall Dive

An hour later, we were suited up to dive the back wall of Molokini. Aaron gave instructions before we entered the water.

"Okay, this dive will be a little different," he said. "It's a drift dive. That means we'll jump in here and the current will carry us along there." He pointed along the back wall.

"You'll feel the current. Captain Andy will follow our bubbles. He'll be in the right spot when it's time for us to come up. Visibility is great—about 150 feet. But you still won't be able to see the bottom.

"Since this is a wall dive, you'll have to keep checking your depth," he continued. "You won't have the ocean floor to tell you where your lowest point is.

"Also, on our last dive, we stayed really close together. That's good. But you'll see more if you spread out a little. As we go along the wall, I'll point out things I see. But look around on your own too. Just don't go too deep," he warned.

"And another thing," he added. "Keep looking out for white-tipped reef sharks. They're down there. If you see one, hold still. I've never known one to attack. They're very shy."

Aaron asked, "Any questions? Okay, remember to keep checking your depth. Let's go."

Aaron jumped into the water. Like baby ducks, we all followed.

As soon as we hit the water, we deflated our bcs and headed to the 50-foot depth. It's hard to describe what we saw.

A steep cliff broke through the silvery surface. It sank into the blue depths. Colorful coral formations grew out of the cliff.

Silver-gold sun rays shone from overhead. Fish of

every color swam about. Even the divers' bubbles were a beautiful, shimmering silver.

The scene was spectacular. My breathing sped up to double time. Aaron led the group along the wall. He pointed out sea life as the current carried us along.

It was easy to flow with the current. But it was a little hard to stop.

Suddenly Aaron motioned for us all to stop. He pointed ahead. A white-tipped reef shark was digging furiously at a ledge. It was about four feet long.

The shark pulled its meal out of the rock. Then it quickly turned and swam off. Dad and I looked at each other wide-eyed. It happened too quickly for Dad to get the picture.

Aaron moved on. He pointed to tiny creatures in the ridges of the wall. Everyone was sticking close together.

I swam away from the group a little. It would be nice to see the little things along the wall. But the total scene was plenty to keep me happy.

What I saw next blew my mind. It looked like the same pearl-colored fish from inside the crater! When our eyes met, it swam away.

Then it circled back and came right up to my face. It swam off again and circled back. I'd never seen a fish act like that. I was pretty sure that the fish wanted me to follow it.

I tried to get Aaron's attention. I wanted him to see the fish's actions. Then later he could explain what was going on. But Aaron had spotted a frogfish and was busy showing it to everyone.

I looked at my dad. He had been watching me like a hawk since we'd reached 50 feet. He was usually right beside or behind me. Right now, though, he was taking pictures of the frogfish.

I looked back at the big pearl-colored fish. It was swimming back and forth.

Did you know a fish's eyes can plead? Well, they can. So I figured it couldn't hurt to follow the fish for a few feet.

As long as everyone was in view, I'd be fine. I'd never felt so sure of anything in my life.

5

Cats

I know when you read this chapter, you're going to think I'm a donut short of a dozen. But keep an open mind until you've read the whole book.

The pearl fish turned and swam along the wall. It went in the direction from which we'd just come. We were swimming against the current. The fish twirled to look at me every few seconds.

At first I had to struggle to keep up. But the swimming got easier. I don't know if the current shifted or if I just got used to it.

Something really strange was happening. My breathing was becoming irregular. I began to hear the most beautiful music I'd ever heard.

Have you ever heard African music where there's a base beat and then voices chanting to another beat? It was kind of like that. I just swam along to the beat. I was really getting into the music.

The pearl fish swam through a crevice in the wall. Without thinking twice, I followed. I couldn't believe how easily I fit. I slipped through the rock more like a fish than like a diver strapped to a tank of air.

I remember thinking that sometimes it pays to be small—and open-minded.

We swam into a huge chamber. It was pearly like the inside of an oyster shell. There were a zillion pinpoints of light shining into the chamber.

We weren't alone for very long. Pretty soon a parade began. Every type of sea creature I'd ever seen—and then some—swam into the chamber.

I guess the best way to explain this is to tell you about *Cats*. My mom took me to see the Broadway play *Cats* when it came to Chicago last year. It was another bonding experience.

Anyway, in *Cats*, different cats tell their stories in song. It sounds weird, but it's really neat.

Well, that's what all these sea creatures did. They put on a Broadway show for me. They danced. They sang. They told me their stories.

They said that the oceans were not our dumping grounds. And that people had better get their act together.

I figured later that I was only gone from the dive group for 10 or 15 minutes. But the show seemed to go on for hours. I didn't want it to end.

But all too soon, it ended. Everything died. It got really ugly.

First the small creatures began to die and decay. Then hollow-eyed fish floated by.

Next, a whale floated past. Its eyes were sunken. Its body was bloated. A swordfish pierced its side. Pus and blood oozed out.

The clear, blue water clouded to brown, then black. The water was thick with junk. It was impossible to see.

I panicked. I wanted out. But I had become too weak to do anything about it.

Then I realized that I was starving. I felt sick. My body went from weak to numb.

The music stopped. My breathing once again became my only sound. It was ragged and irregular.

The show was over.

6

The Message

I could have easily died right then. Instead, the water cleared and I felt better.

Have you ever been really sick? Remember that great feeling when you begin to recover? The sun shines brighter and everything seems sweeter. That's how I felt.

So I floated around in the chamber. I was too full of questions and too worn out to be worried about being lost.

The pearl fish swam toward me. Its eyes searched mine. I hung in the water, recovering and staring at the fish. It seemed like we floated that way for a long time.

Slowly, a message began to form. It didn't form in my head. And the fish didn't actually speak. But the message was clear.

If the seas die, we all die. Tell them.

I blinked my understanding. The fish did a little bow and swam through the crevice. I followed. As soon as I swam through the crack, the fish was gone.

I drifted with the current for a few minutes. I relived the experience in my mind. I didn't want to forget any details.

After a while, I checked my computer. I had gone to 65 feet. And I had only 120 psi in my tank.

I looked around for my dive group. They weren't in sight. But that didn't bother me. In fact, I was amazingly calm. I guess after what I'd just been through, this didn't seem like such a big deal.

I decided to swim with the current. I made sure my bubbles rose a little faster than I did. I rose slowly. And I checked my computer as I went.

At 20 feet, I did a safety stop. I checked my computer to see how much air I had. There was 60 psi left. That was cutting it really close.

In the distance, I saw two divers rising quickly. They didn't perform a safety stop. For the first time since I'd followed the fish, I thought about Dad.

I broke the surface and saw the dive boat. The two divers were being helped aboard. I blew air into my bc until I was buoyant. Then I started waving my arms and shouting.

After a minute, the boat began moving toward me.

7

On Deck

I saw people scurrying around as the boat neared. When it got closer, I counted five heads. There should have been seven.

I wasn't worried, though. I was feeling pretty puffed up. I carried an important message. That was all I could think about.

The boat pulled alongside me. Captain Andy grabbed me by my bc and hauled me on board. In seconds, he had removed my gear.

In his booming voice, he ordered me to lie on the deck. Dad and Aaron were already sprawled out. They were breathing oxygen.

Dad half sat up when he saw me. He looked weak. And he was shaking.

When he saw that I was okay, he lay back down again. Pretty soon somebody slapped oxygen on my face too.

Captain Andy leaned over me. Bent over like that, his red face hung around his eyes and cheekbones like the flesh of a rotting fish. I thought about how similar living things are.

"How do you feel? Did you do a decompression stop? You were down too long. Your computer says you went too deep. Did something go wrong?"

I looked into Captain Andy's eyes. It took me a minute to focus on them because his face was hidden in the sun's shadow. But when I did, I saw concern—and disgust.

"Fine. Yes. I know. No," I answered as best I could. I did feel a little dizzy. The sun kept peeking over Captain Andy's shoulder into my eyes. And the boat was rocking.

I turned my head to see Dad looking at me. He looked concerned. Suddenly, guilt ran through my whole body like an icy hand grabbing and squeezing my insides.

Then the icy hand gripped down and squeezed *everything* out. I turned away from Dad. Quickly, I jerked the oxygen off. Then I spewed the contents of my stomach onto the deck.

Captain Andy straightened up like an old man. He walked to his radio. One of the other divers was steering the boat toward shore. Everybody was quiet.

Someone washed my vomit overboard with a bucket of seawater. I fell asleep.

In my dream, the pearl fish swam toward me. It opened its mouth, and I swam in. The fish was full of cool water. It felt great.

I didn't want to leave. But someone was trying to pull me out. A voice was buzzing at me. And it wasn't the beautiful sound of the ocean.

I opened my eyes. There was Captain Andy again.

On my other side, a woman in a gray jumpsuit was leaning over me. "Wake up, Jon. Look at me. Look at me, Jon," she commanded.

I looked at her. I saw my dad standing behind the woman. Dad looked pretty good—except for the worry on his face.

Aaron was standing beside Dad. He looked okay too. I couldn't figure out why they were all staring at me.

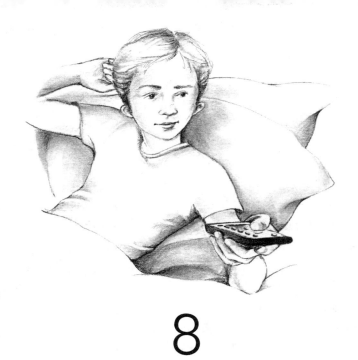

8

Later

A few hours later, we were back in our hotel room. We were drinking soda and watching TV.

Aaron, Dad, and I had all checked out okay in the emergency room. But they warned us to take it easy for at least 24 hours.

All I'd told Dad was that I got lost following an interesting fish. Dad leaned over from his bed and poked my shoulder with a finger.

"I can't figure how you disappeared so fast," he said. "I just turned around and you were gone. What made you follow that fish? And how did you get lost along a wall?"

What was I going to say? The fish was pleading with me so I followed it into a hole in the crater?

"It just looked interesting, Dad," I said instead. "I must have followed it farther than I realized."

Dad laughed and asked, "Did this fish have long hair and beautiful blue eyes? That's called a *mermaid*, son."

I was quiet. Then he brought up the subject I'd been waiting for. The doctor who checked me out in the emergency room had brought it up first.

"You probably had nitrogen narcosis," Dad said. "Remember what that is? We learned about it in our diving lessons."

"Yeah," I said. "It's like getting high. The deeper you go, the higher you get. But it usually doesn't happen under 100 feet. You know I didn't go that deep. I didn't go as deep as you did. And I wasn't high."

"It must have been nitrogen narcosis. How else could you get lost along a wall?" Dad looked sure of himself.

"You lose your judgment," Dad continued. "And you can hallucinate. You know, diving affects different people in different ways. You're small. And you're an inexperienced diver. The depth probably affected you."

I had to think about that. It couldn't have been nitrogen narcosis. Could it?

I was pretty sure I hadn't hallucinated. It had been too real. And what about the message? I hadn't imagined that.

I quit talking. Now I knew if I told Dad what I'd seen and heard, he'd definitely claim nitrogen narcosis.

While we were waiting at the hospital, Aaron had told me what happened when I was underwater. He said that when I disappeared so quickly, he sent the other divers up. He and Dad had stayed down, looking for me. Dad wouldn't surface when it was time. So they ran out of air underwater.

Aaron carried a can of pressurized air. He and Dad had shared the can when their air ran out.

Still, they rose too quickly. They didn't have enough air to make a safety stop. So they had bobbed to the surface. They had been in danger of getting the bends.

Dad's plan had been to get a fresh tank and go right back down. I guess he thought I'd gotten caught on a rock or attacked by a shark or something. But just as they climbed aboard, one of the other divers spotted me.

I was thinking back on all of this when Dad leaned over and threw me a curve. He said, "One thing I know for sure, Jon. Our diving days are over."

"Sure, maybe this trip," I agreed. "But we'll dive again. I loved it, Dad. You really can trust me. I was responsible down there after I realized that I was lost."

Dad looked at me. "No next time. We're through. I'm not risking your life again. I wish I'd never had the idea to learn how to scuba dive," he said.

I felt like I'd been punched in the stomach. I couldn't remember ever having done anything that I liked so much. And now I'd been given a message. I had a mission. I was sure it would include future diving.

I pleaded, "Dad, it was great—beautiful. I'll admit I wasn't all that crazy about taking all the classes. But I loved it down there today. I want to go again."

Dad just looked at me. "When you're an adult, you can do what you want. Until then, you're done."

That made me really mad at Dad. I just hoped he'd change his mind. I couldn't imagine not diving. And I knew that an Illinois teenager would have a hard time diving without some kind of parental help.

Dad dozed on and off for the rest of the afternoon. I just channel-surfed. I felt fine. Along with a bunch of other emotions, I was excited about my mission. I sat there thinking about it and flicking through the stations.

Dad woke up about 6:00. We ordered from room

service. They sent up huge hamburgers with everything, fries, coleslaw, and key lime pie for dessert.

We ate in the room and watched the old movie *Waterworld*. Dad thought the movie stunk. I, of course, loved it.

After the movie, Dad fell asleep again. He seemed to be sleeping an awful lot.

I finally fell asleep. And there was the pearl fish. It was swimming along with me in the deep blue waters of the ocean.

It was about three in the morning when Dad woke up with a pain in his left shoulder. He said later that his arm felt numb. At first, he thought it might be a heart attack. That's when he woke me.

I fumbled for the light switch. "What's the matter?" I asked.

"Pain. Bad pain," Dad gasped. "Call 911. I'm probably bent."

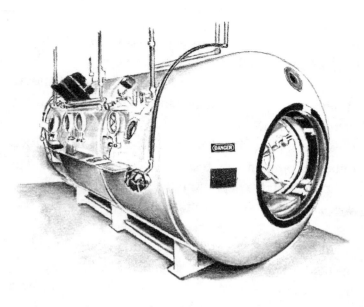

9

Tiny Bubbles

I dialed the number. In no time, we were on our way to the local hospital.

They did a neurological exam and agreed that Dad had the bends. They put him in a hyperbaric chamber. Dr. Kahana said the pain would go away after Dad went through the hyperbaric therapy.

Then Dr. Kahana examined me. He was much more thorough than the guy in the emergency room earlier.

"You know," said Dr. Kahana, "the deeper you go, the greater the pressure. Since your dad rose so fast, his lungs didn't get rid of the nitrogen gas he took in going down."

Dr. Kahana checked my reflexes. "When your dad surfaced," he continued, "the nitrogen started turning to tiny bubbles in his blood. He's lucky it settled in his shoulder. It could have settled in his brain and killed him.

"So, in effect, we're sending him back down by reapplying pressure. Then we'll bring him to normal pressure slowly so his body can adjust. We'll keep him on pure oxygen while he's undergoing therapy. He's got about five hours to go."

Dr. Kahana looked at me. "Your dad said that you were down for a long time too. He asked me to check you out."

I was kind of a mess at that point. Dad could have died because of me.

"I know I'm fine," I told Dr. Kahana. "I came up slowly. And I did a stop."

Dr. Kahana said, "Your dad told me you had nitrogen narcosis. You may have thought you did a stop. Of course, we can't tell now whether you actually had nitrogen narcosis. It disappears as you rise to the surface. But decompression sickness doesn't go away so easily."

I tested out fine. But I wished it had been me with the bends.

10

The Recovery

That afternoon, Dad and I went back to the hotel. Some vacation! We could have stayed home and gone to the hospital.

At least Dad was feeling better. He had spent six hours in the hyperbaric chamber. He was supposed to relax and drink lots of liquids.

Of course, Dr. Kahana had said that diving was out for the rest of the vacation. That was just fine with Dad.

We found some beach chairs and got comfortable. Dad ordered a couple of papaya-guava drinks. Then he pulled out a paperback. He opened the book and removed the little umbrella from his drink. Finally, he settled back to relax.

"This is the life, huh, Jon?" Dad said. "Look at this scenery. Blue-green water, blue sky, white sand, bikinis as bright as those fish we saw yesterday. Add a good book, and what more could we want?"

To be in the water, I thought. I sighed. I felt like an old man sitting in the beach chair. I looked around. Most of our lawn-chair buddies looked like my grandparents.

Everybody young was on the beach. I knew, though, that I owed Dad a lot. The very least I could do was stay with him. So I sat and watched the scenery.

After a while, I realized that Dad was deep into his book. He didn't seem to need my company.

"Would you mind if I went for a little walk?"

"Okay," Dad said, "but don't let any mermaids lure you into the water." He laughed and burrowed back into his book.

I walked along the shore. The waves lapped at my bare feet. Just a short distance down the beach, I saw snorkelers. I figured that there must be more than sand under the water here—maybe some coral or a wreck.

I decided I'd ask Dad if I could bring my mask, snorkel, and fins tomorrow. It wasn't scuba diving, but at least I'd be in the water.

I walked back along the beach. For an instant, I heard that beautiful music I'd heard the morning before. It made me want to jump into the ocean.

I did wade out a little. Then the sound was gone. I stopped and wondered what was going on.

That night, Dad and I walked up the road to a seafood restaurant. At dinner, I asked Dad if he thought we should call Mom and tell her what had happened.

"Let's not worry her. We'll tell her when we get home. We're okay now. Let's just leave it at that," Dad said.

"Sounds good," I said. "I want to tell Mom, though, that *I* messed up. And you did everything you could. You even risked your own neck to save me. I think she should know that."

"I messed up trying to save you," Dad half whispered. "And I messed up losing sight of you down there. I should never have taken my eyes off you.

"Your mom wasn't all that crazy about you taking scuba in the first place. She knows how dangerous diving can be. She just went along with it because it gave you and me a bond. I have a feeling that when she learns what happened, she'll never let me take you anywhere again."

This was getting heavy. But there were some things I needed to say to Dad. So I cleared my throat and said, "Dad, that was all my fault. When Mom hears the whole story, she'll think you're a hero."

I paused and then continued, "I haven't even said 'thanks.' And I haven't told you I love you for about five years. But I do."

"I love you too, son," Dad said. Then he lightened up and changed the subject. He suggested we pay the check and go see what was on the tube for the evening.

When we got back to the room, he was out like a light in about half an hour. I fell asleep wondering how I was going to accomplish this mission I'd been given.

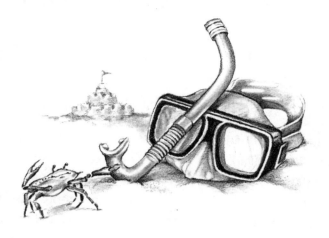

11

Snorkeling

Late the next morning, Dad and I headed back down to the water. Dad had agreed that I could snorkel. He followed me down the beach to the snorkeling spot.

With his paperback and a bottle of spring water, Dad seemed content. And he seemed to have a little more pep than the day before. That really made me feel better.

I had my snorkel, mask, fins, and Dad's underwater camera. He said I might as well get some use out of it.

I set off toward the water. I promised to check back in an hour. We both wore our new dive watches. We had synchronized them. Dad was really serious about my checking in.

I thought it was kind of funny because he could see me from his position on the beach. And, if I went under and he was really involved in his book, he wouldn't know it until it was way too late. But I went along with it. I guess it made him feel a little more in control.

The water felt cool and soothing. My body had adjusted to it by the time I was in up to my waist. I pulled on my fins and swam. The camera was strapped to my left arm.

The bottom was sandy for several yards. A few colorful fish swam by. All of a sudden, there was a ridge. The bottom was covered with coral.

I found out later that the coral was attached to lava flows from Haleakala. They had been formed hundreds—or maybe thousands—of years ago.

I swam around, looking at the undersea garden. Once in a while, I'd dive down for a close-up snapshot of a fish or some coral. It was easy not to go too far out. When the water became too deep, I swam in toward the beach.

It felt so good to have the sun on my back and the cool water beneath me. It made me feel part of both environments. Lying there, floating above the fish and coral, I knew that I wanted to make the ocean my life's work.

I floated for some time. Then I looked at my dive watch. It was time to report to Dad.

"Hey, right on time!" Dad seemed impressed. "I guess you didn't run into any mermaids today." He laughed again. Why do dads love to tease their kids with the same stale, corny jokes?

"You should see what's out there, Dad," I said. "It's as beautiful as what we saw at Molokini. Don't you want to snorkel just a little? It really doesn't take a lot of effort. And you're not diving deep. The salt water buoys you up. All you have to do is move your fins once in a while."

Know what he said? "I'll just look at your pictures. Actually, I think I've seen enough ocean to last the rest of my life."

I couldn't believe how he could just get over the ocean like that. I mean, here's this gorgeous underwater treasure that neither of us had ever seen firsthand before. And now he didn't even want to put on a mask and look at it.

"You know, all this sitting around has made me hungry," Dad said. "How about we get some lunch?"

Now *that* I could agree with.

12

The Promise

By early afternoon, I was on my way back down the beach to the water. I'd eaten a big lunch with Dad. Then I'd sat with him for another hour. I'd kept him company while the sun toasted the front of my body.

My back was getting plenty of sun as I snorkeled. And I'm vain enough to not want to look like an Oreo with the top off. So I figured I could even out my tan while keeping Dad happy.

Dad had slathered sunblock on himself. He really thought I should do the same. So I let him put some on my back.

I described the coral formations that were right under the waves in front of us. I was anxious to get back to them.

I told Dad I wanted to get some books on ocean life. I wanted to find out more about the corals and the various kinds of fish. He seemed impressed with my enthusiasm.

Finally, I put my mask, snorkel, and fins back on. I dove into the waves. A little chill ran through me. But soon the water felt refreshing again on my warm skin.

I swam out toward the coral. This time I left the camera behind. I'd taken some pictures before. Now I wanted to look at things up close with my own eyes.

Almost immediately, I heard that sweet music again. It was the same music that I thought I'd heard the day before. I began to glide through the water in time to the beat.

Strangely, I didn't feel any sense of doom this time. I felt peaceful. I just swam along to that great music.

I dove deep and came face-to-face with the pearl fish. As the fish's eye met mine, I thought I can't follow you. Immediately, I knew that the fish understood.

I floated back to the surface so that I could breathe through my snorkel. The fish stayed right with me. It looked me straight in the eye. We swam along slowly—never breaking eye contact.

Suddenly, I quit swimming. I just lay there on the surface of the water. I stared at the pearl fish for the longest time.

This time, *I* sent the message. Well, it wasn't really another message. If the first message had been an invitation, then this message was the RSVP. This message was from me to the fish.

I promise.

I blinked and the fish swam off. I watched it grow smaller and smaller until the water ate it up.

I lay on the water. I thought about the wonders of the ocean. The beauty, knowledge, history, and future that lay within my sight were awesome. The music had faded away—but not really. It had become part of my memory and part of me.

As I floated along like this, someone tapped me on the shoulder. I raised my head and pulled down my mask.

A man asked, "Are you okay? Your dad was worried because you didn't seem to be moving."

I shot Dad an OK signal and told the man I was fine. I wasn't quite ready to go in yet. So I swam around for a while.

I thought about the message and my feelings about it. Then, when I was ready, I swam toward shore.

13

The Talk

Dad sat in his beach chair. He looked like he was involved in his novel. I knew, though, that he'd been watching every move I made.

"Oh, hi. You're back already." He glanced up from his book.

"Yeah, I've seen every fish in the ocean now," I joked. "Some twice. And your friend woke me up from my nap."

"No more mermaids?" Dad asked for what seemed like the hundredth time.

I decided to tell Dad the whole story. In a way, I had proof now. Seeing the pearl fish again was proof that I hadn't imagined it yesterday.

Besides, I was too excited to keep it inside. I needed to talk.

"Actually, Dad, I did see that fish again—the one I followed when we were at Molokini. It gave me a message at Molokini. And I just gave it a message back."

Dad snorted. Then he saw the look on my face. "What was the message, Jon?"

"I know you won't believe this happened, but it did. It really did. It's the biggest thing that's ever happened to me. And I plan to carry through with it."

I told him step-by-step everything that had happened at Molokini. Then I described what had happened while I was snorkeling. Finally, I told him what I had promised.

Dad listened. Then he leaned his head back. He gazed toward that line where the sky meets the sea.

He sat that way for a long time. I began to think he'd fallen asleep. Finally, he looked at me and asked, "How are you supposed to do that?"

"I don't know yet. I don't know how I'll do it. It's kind of like the oceans chose me to spread the message about what we're doing to the earth."

Dad let out a long sigh and closed his eyes again. "I agree with the message, Jon. But don't you think you already had that information? Maybe you do want to help keep the oceans clean. But don't you think you could have given yourself the message?"

I should have known he'd say that. I sat down on the beach towel. I needed for him to know that I hadn't been experiencing nitrogen narcosis. I told him my story again.

Even as I was talking, I knew it wouldn't matter how much detail I went into. Dad wasn't going to believe me—no matter what. I was ready for what was coming next.

"Okay, Jon," Dad said. "Let's get this straight. Two days ago at Molokini, this white fish and a cast of thousands performed a 'destruction of the oceans' skit for you. Then the fish asked you to promise to save the oceans and all creatures of the earth in the process. And today it swam from Molokini Crater to this beach. And you told it that you would keep the promise."

He looked at me with disbelieving eyes.

"I really don't know how far a fish would swim," he continued. "But I think they have their territories. And you know, of course, what tiny brains fish have. You think this fish could learn your language, track you all over the ocean, and give *you* the message to save the world? You are only 14, you know. If the fish is so smart, why wouldn't it choose someone with a little more power?"

"Dad, this fish seemed more like a 'spokesfish.' It didn't look like any fish I've ever seen. I don't know how it did it. Maybe it was programmed by some whales or dolphins. They're really smart." Even as I spoke, I knew I was sounding like a lunatic.

Dad just sat and looked at me. He rubbed his forehead and said, "I think when we get home, I'll have you talk with Dave Young. Maybe this divorce has been harder on you than we thought. Maybe you should talk to someone."

I sat there with my mouth hanging open. Dr. Young is a golf buddy of Dad's. He's also a psychiatrist.

14

Mom

Two days later, I was sitting in the living room with Mom and Dad. We had just told Mom about the trip. Mom seemed to take the whole thing pretty well. The color drained out of her face a couple of times. But she didn't faint or yell or anything.

Then Dad asked me to explain why I'd become lost on the dive trip. I told Mom the whole story just as I had told it to Dad. When I was finished, Mom leaned back and looked at Dad. Then she let out a sigh.

"You know, Alex, I think it might be good if just Jon and I talk about this. Are you okay now?" Mom asked.

"I'm fine," Dad answered. "No effects from the airplane ride—just a little jet lag. I'm pretty sure the hyperbaric chamber fixed me. Call me," he said to Mom and stood up to leave.

Dad came over and patted me on the shoulder. "I think we can keep you away from that fish here. See you soon, kid."

After Dad left, Mom leaned forward. She looked at me and smiled. "Tell me the whole thing again, will you, honey? I want to make sure I've got this all straight."

So I told the story once more. Dad had asked for all the details again on the flight home. I wondered if they would compare notes.

After the second retelling, I asked Mom if she believed me.

"Sure, I believe you, honey." She smiled at me. "It's wonderful that you've found a cause to fight for," she said. "It certainly is a worthwhile one."

I smiled back at her. I could tell she didn't believe me. I stood up.

"I'm gonna go see Carlos," I told her.

"Don't you want to rest first?" she asked. "That was a long flight."

"I'm okay."

I meant that in every possible way.

As soon as I left, Mom probably called Dad. Then one of them called Dr. Young to make an appointment.

15

Vacation Pictures

I told Carlos the whole story. We were walking to the bike trail where we roller blade.

"Sure, I believe you," Carlos said as he laced up his blades. "Sounds way cool. Wish I could learn to scuba. Wish I could go to Hawaii."

I decided to go with it. I needed all the support I could get. I don't have to jump through hoops to prove things to Carlos.

"I just wish my parents believed me," I said. "They're going to have me talk to a psychiatrist. Like I'm psycho or something."

"You're not nuts. A little weird maybe," Carlos joked. "I think it sounds cool to get to talk to a psychiatrist. Know what that costs? You're lucky!"

I finished lacing up my blades. Just as I was standing up, Carlos yelled, "Race!" He took off.

I followed as quickly as I could. Between the jet lag and being off roller blades for over a week, I had some catching up to do.

A couple of days later, Mom and I were at Dr. Young's office. He talked to my mom first.

"Karen, I would like you here today," he told her. "But next time, I'd like Jon to come alone. I know that Alex is interested in participating too. But this is a matter for Jon to sort out. We'll call you both in if we need you."

Dr. Young turned his attention to me. "Now, Jon," he said. "Please tell me why you are here."

So I told the story of the message once more. Dr. Young listened. He nodded once in a while. He didn't say whether he believed me or not.

When I got home after my first shrink session, there was a phone message from Dad. He was coming over with six packets of pictures from the trip.

We sat down and started opening packets. About two-thirds of the pictures were of me. There were only a couple pictures of Dad.

Almost everything we did on the trip was recorded in photos—except the emergency room visits. I guess that's where I could have been taking pictures. Dad in the ambulance. Dad in the hyperbaric chamber. Oh well, those were probably things he really didn't want pictures of anyway.

"Look at this one of you surrounded by those butterfly fish," Dad said as he passed it to me.

I looked at the picture closely. There it was! The big pearl fish was in the background. It was almost hidden behind the yellow butterfly fish. But it was looking at me as I looked at the camera. I showed it to Dad.

"That's it. That's the fish I followed. That's the fish that gave me the message!" Dad leaned over to look. He stared at the picture for a long time. Then he looked at me.

Quickly, he dug through the pile of pictures. "Here's another," he said. He handed me a picture of just me and the fish.

"I didn't realize you meant *that* fish," Dad said. "I didn't see it on the second dive, but I remember it on the first dive. It was following you pretty closely. I took this picture because I'd never seen a fish pay that much attention to a person before." His voice trailed off.

"I wonder what kind of fish it is," he said after a moment of silence.

16

The Spokesfish

After he saw the picture of the fish, Dad began to treat me a little differently. He hasn't said he believes me yet. And I'm pretty sure he still thinks I had nitrogen narcosis.

But seeing the picture of the fish changed something. He didn't act as if I were completely crazy anymore. Maybe he was considering the possibilities . . .

I had a poster made from one of the pictures of the fish. It's hanging in my room as a reminder of what I'm about.

When I lie in bed and stare at that poster, I see a big pearl fish that looks like it's posing for a picture. I'm not kidding. It looks like the fish actually knew Dad was capturing it on film.

Here's another thing. I checked books about the fish that live around Hawaii. I couldn't find that fish. So I started searching through books on all kinds of fish.

I'm not sure if I've found the exact fish. But I did find a cold-water fish that looks like it. The book said that the fish is very tasty. It's a main food in the diets of people in northern countries. Because of overfishing, though, the fish has become a threatened species. I'm pretty sure that's my fish.

I showed the information about the fish to Dad. He agreed that the picture did look pretty similar to the fish on my poster.

He said, "If the fish was being fished into extinction, it probably took off to escape. It may have adapted to warmer waters out of necessity. Maybe no one knows the fish is in the tropics. That might be of interest to someone."

Yeah, I thought. The people who like to eat it. I decided not to tell anyone.

I showed the poster to Carlos.

"That fish looks smart, man," he said. "Look at that huge forehead. That fish has a brain. I bet it could send messages."

Good old Carlos.

I showed the poster to a couple of other friends too. But I didn't tell them about the message. At that point, I didn't think everyone needed to know *where* I got the message. I just needed them to get the message from me.

17

Thank you, Dr. Y.

I had a few more visits with Dr. Young. By this time, I called him *Dr. Y.* Here's a typical conversation from one of our sessions.

"So, how are you today, Jon?"

"Fine. I'm getting pretty bored with summer, though."

"What do you mean by that, Jon?"

"Well, there isn't much to do. I really like to keep busy. I've been thinking that next year I'll get a job."

"What kind of job would you like, Jon?"

Get the picture? I could have had this same conversation for free with my Aunt Trudy.

But Mom and Dad wanted to spend money on me. It made them feel better. So I talked with Dr. Y.

My next-to-last session was the best, though. Dr. Y. actually talked to me instead of just asking me questions. Two good things happened.

First, I found out that Dr. Y. has a son named Tad. He's in college and scuba dives. Dr. Y. said that maybe sometime he and his son and Dad and I could go on a scuba trip.

I thought that was pretty cool of him. With Dr. Y. and a little time on my side, Mom and Dad might give in.

And the other thing was the idea I got from the newspaper. I told Dr. Y. about it. He thought it was an excellent idea. He suggested I do a little research and see where that led.

So I did. And it led to really good things.

My last meeting with Dr. Y. included a meeting with Mom and Dad. Dr. Y. told them that I'm not psychotic. He said I may have possibly experienced a hallucination. But it doesn't seem to have been harmful.

In fact, he said, it appears to have given me some direction. He told my parents they were lucky to have a son who knows what he wants to do.

After that little talk, my parents dropped the whole subject. We don't discuss the message anymore. In fact, we haven't had a lot of time to talk lately. We've all been too busy.

18

The First Issue

This past fall, I joined the Environmental Action Club at school. When I joined, there were only eight members. Then I got all my friends and a few others to join. That more than tripled the membership.

I volunteered to be co-president too. Which means that the other co-president and I have done most of the work. But we don't mind. We like each other's company. And with that many members, we can usually find help.

That fall, the club got involved in an issue. It was the one Dr. Y. had suggested I research. I had read about the issue in the newspaper one morning last summer.

I had been doing my front-page glance of the newspaper when a headline caught my eye.

The article said that surrounding states had enforced tough laws on large-scale hog farms. It said that these large hog farms were like factories. They were polluting the environment.

The odor was one problem. Everyone knows that hogs don't exactly smell fresh and clean.

But manure storage was the biggest problem. The hog manure was stored in football field-sized lagoons. The article said that it wasn't unusual for a lagoon to burst.

There was a big spill a few years ago. It leaked 22 million gallons of hog manure into a nearby river. It killed fish 20 miles downstream.

Manure runoff was another concern. The manure in the lagoons was used as fertilizer. It was spread on the fields by huge manure guns that shoot the liquid manure 50 feet into the air.

There was often runoff because too much liquid manure was applied. It ended up in nearby streams, ponds, and drainage lines.

The runoff could harm the soil too. The minerals in hog manure are very strong.

Here in the middle of the country, we had a water-quality issue. I live on the Mississippi River—the biggest river in the country. So the manure runoff could be in our water.

And, if hog poop goes into the Mississippi, it would end up in the Gulf of Mexico. And that's part of the ocean.

That's where my message began.

19

Charly

When Dr. Y. suggested I do some research, I took his advice. So that afternoon, I rode my bike to the main library. I found some articles on hog farming and settled down at a table.

I chose a particular table because Charleen Van Deventer was sitting at it. She had been new at school that spring. I'd noticed her, but we'd never spoken.

Charleen Van Deventer isn't the kind of girl you can just go up to and say "hi." She's too beautiful—too perfect. She's already the height I hope to be some day. She has long, curly red hair and green eyes like emeralds. Her smooth ivory skin is like silk.

I sat down across the table from her. She didn't look up. I took out my notebook. I started taking notes.

Every once in a while, I'd glance up. She just kept her nose in the book. This went on for over an hour. By that time, I'd taken a lot of notes.

I needed to go find another resource. But I was afraid she'd leave before I got back. Finally, I just sat there and stared at her.

It worked. In about a minute, she looked up. I stood up and held out my hand.

"Hi, I'm Jon Olivera," I said. "We go to school together."

She shook my hand and smiled. "I'm Charly."

"You just moved here last spring, didn't you?"

"Yeah," she whispered. "We moved from Iowa."

Without thinking, I blurted out, "Your dad isn't a big hog farmer, is he?" My face must have turned beet red under my tan. I wanted to kick myself.

"No," she said. "He works for the phone company."

"I'm studying factory farms," I explained. I hoped she didn't think I was a complete idiot.

"Interesting," she said. "What are you going to do with the information?"

"I don't know for sure yet. I'm going to try and stop them—or fix the problems—or something." I told her what problems the manure lagoons caused. It was kind of hard to talk about pig poop with someone so pretty.

Remember earlier when I said that I have a big voice? Evidently, I was using it. A librarian came over and asked me to whisper or leave. I turned that into an opportunity.

"I'm thirsty. Are you?"

"A little," she said.

"Do you want to get something to drink?" I asked. I couldn't believe I was asking Charleen Van Deventer to get a drink with *me*.

"Sure, I guess," she replied.

We walked to a bagel place across the street. We ordered our drinks and sat down.

I was surprised that Charly was so easy to talk with. I wondered why I'd waited so long to get to know her.

"What are you studying at the library?" I finally asked her.

"I went back to Iowa for a couple of weeks. My grandma got me thinking about ancestors. So I've been doing some research on the Van Deventers."

"Will you be coming back to the library?" I asked.

"Yes."

"When?" I persisted.

"Tomorrow." Charly smiled.

"I'm gonna be there myself," I said. "What time will you be there?"

"About the same time," Charly said.

"I'll probably see you then," I said. I knew there was no "probably" about it. I definitely planned on being there.

Charly smiled.

20

More Charly

I couldn't believe my luck! For a long time, I'd been watching Charleen Van Deventer. And I wasn't alone. All the guys had been watching her. I guess everybody felt the same way I had—that she was too beautiful to speak to.

After talking to her, though, I realized how shy she was. People probably mistook her shyness for an attitude. I know I had.

The next day, I went to the library right after lunch. Right before lunch, I'd showered and splashed on a little aftershave. Too bad there was no shave for it to come after.

At the library, I looked through some newspaper articles. I kept glancing at the table to see if Charly was there yet.

The night before, I had looked up hog manure on the Internet. I found that I could get lots of information there. But now I had a special reason to use the library.

At about 2:10, Charly came in. She grabbed a book from a shelf and sat down. I walked coolly over to her table. That was hard to do. I wanted to sprint.

Behind her, I saw the library lady glaring at me. I put my finger up to my lips and raised my eyebrows at her. With a little frown, she looked away.

Charly glanced up and smiled. I felt like I was in slow motion. Finally, I reached her table. I leaned over and whispered very quietly, "Would you like to go for a walk along the river in about an hour? We could get some ice cream."

She nodded and smiled. Charleen Van Deventer actually smiled at me! I practically skipped back to my newspaper. The next hour seemed like ten years.

Finally, we left the library. We walked along the river, learning more about each other.

I told Charly about my diving trip with my dad. I told her about the hyperbaric chamber. But I didn't tell her about the fish. I wasn't sure how she would react.

Right now, I wanted to impress her. Later, I'd tell her about the fish. Of course, I didn't tell her about Dr. Y. either.

I did say that the diving trip had made me seriously interested in oceanography. But since I didn't live near any oceans, I decided that I'd begin with the water quality in my own area.

We bought ice-cream cones at a little shop. Then we sat on a bench and watched the Mississippi flow by.

My thoughts jumped back and forth. First I thought, Wow! I'm sitting here with Charleen Van Deventer! Then I wondered how much pollution was in the Mississippi River.

Those thoughts weren't equal, of course. There were about three or four "Wow!" thoughts for every Mississippi thought.

Charly finally broke the silence. She turned to me and said, "I'm getting a little bored with family history."

Don't say that! I thought. That would mean no more library.

"Could you use some help?" she asked me. "I'm really interested in what you're doing. I'd like to get involved."

I took the last bite of my cone and turned to her. "Sure," I said in an offhand manner. But my heart was beating wildly.

21

The Environmental Action Club

In less than a week, we were holding hands and kissing.

This is the first relationship that I've had with a girl that's based on friendship and mutual interests. That's probably why it's lasting so long.

Of course, it's more than a friendship. I'm really attracted to Charly. And she seems to be attracted to me— even though I'm four inches shorter.

When some of the more jock-type guys saw me with her, they tried to horn in. She let them know she wasn't interested.

So anyway, Charly and I spent the last two weeks of summer researching pig poop. We learned a lot about the ins and outs of hog farming—especially the mega type. We pretty much looked through every reference in the library.

And we checked the Internet together. That was nice—sharing a chair and reading the screen together. She ran the mouse. I typed on the keyboard.

We didn't really research all the time. But it was a great excuse to be together.

Charly roller blades too. So she and Carlos and I have spent a lot of time on wheels. Sometimes we did our best thinking on roller blades.

When school started, Charly and I met with Ms. Mason. She was the sponsor of the Environmental Action Club. We told her about our plans.

She helped us call the first meeting of the club. This was strange since neither of us had been members the year before. She said it would be great to have some members who were really "gung ho."

The club members showed up, along with my friends. All the members seemed happy to have two volunteer leaders and an issue to work on. We assigned certain people to monitor the TV news, the local newspaper, the legislature, and the county board.

Charly and I presented highlights of our research. Some of our presentation got a few laughs. It also got the club members mad. And it made them excited about working toward change.

It was scary to think that such a health hazard could go unchecked if it weren't for a few concerned citizens. We planned to be those citizens.

Twice as many kids showed up for our second meeting. We went on a field trip to a factory farm.

The best way to learn was through real-life, hands-on experience. Fortunately, in this case, there was no actual hands-on experience. But we did fill our noses with enough memories to last a long, long time.

Dad helped with the field trip. We needed rides, so several parents volunteered. Mom and Dad seemed glad that I'd turned my "episode" into an asset.

Dad actually got pretty involved. He helped us contact important people. Later, he drove us to some hearings. He even sat through all the testimony.

Over the next couple of months, we did everything we could to raise awareness of the mega-farm threat. We didn't do anything crazy.

You know how the PETA (People for the Ethical Treatment of Animals) people have been known to throw red paint on people wearing fur? Well, we didn't throw hog poop on anybody.

We wrote letters to the editor. We made posters and hung them in stores and public places. We carried signs at football games. Carlos even rented a pig costume to wear to a game.

The pig costume was such a hit that we decided to have a Halloween Pig Parade. We all dressed up in pig stuff and carried signs.

Some just had masks. Some wore all pink. One guy borrowed a baby pig from his uncle who was a farmer. He pushed the piglet in a buggy. I went as Super Swine, cape and all.

Charly went as Miss Piggy. She had on a pig snout, a tiara, a fancy dress from a secondhand store, and one of those feather boa things. She didn't look anything like Miss Piggy. But she got lots of attention anyway.

We carried signs that said things like "Pigs need their space!" "Boycott bacon!" and "We're drowning in pig poop!" We passed out information flyers too.

That was the night we learned that you need a permit to have a parade. They didn't arrest us. But we had to stay on the sidewalks and just walk around neighborhoods. We probably couldn't have even done that if it hadn't been Trick-or-Treat night.

It turned out okay. We got the message out to lots of people. And we had a blast in the process.

Later, we all went to the Pancake Place in our pig costumes. We ordered stacks of pancakes without bacon, ham, or sausage. The staff thought that was pretty funny.

If the seas die,
we all die.
Tell them.

22

Hog Hoopla

It's been a great year. It's been exciting and interesting. A year ago, I never would have thought I'd be so interested in pig poop because a fish spoke to me. And I never would have imagined that I'd have Charleen Van Deventer for a girlfriend—pretty much because a fish spoke to me.

It goes to show you never know what's around the corner—or in the crater.

All the hog hoopla was because of the legislature. They had passed a bill called the Livestock Waste Management Facilities Act. The main problem was that the bill was too weak to really protect the environment. If you read it, you might think the mega-farmers had written it.

People were mad because the bill was weak. From what I understand, people in some other states had been going through the same thing.

Of course, the media got involved. There were lots of news reports and articles on the issue.

I've been thinking about going into journalism. You have the freedom to look at an issue from the outside. That'd be cool.

Hearings were held to find out how the laws should be strengthened. Several members of the Environmental Action Club testified. We also wrote our legislators. While the hearings were in progress, the state temporarily stopped new hog confinement mega-farms.

By the way, this whole mega-farm deal hasn't been just about hogs. It's about cattle too. They take up even more space than hogs do. And anybody who's ever been to a farm knows how big a cow pie is.

The good thing about all the hearings was that tighter laws were formed for the regulation of the mega-farms. It's a big deal to build a lagoon now. You need engineers, geologists, liners in the lagoons, soil testing, periodic groundwater testing, and all kinds of other stuff.

I didn't expect people to quit eating pork. But I had hoped for something more than what we got.

Sure, the new laws have made it harder to build a mega-farm. But that didn't stop the pork producers. They're still building them. But at least they're safer. And we'll keep watching them.

I've learned that being a real environmentalist is a never-ending battle. It takes a lot of work and a long time to create change. That's why I keep the poster of the fish in my room.

Last week, I finally showed Charly the poster. I told her about the message—and about Dr. Y. Know what she said?

"I figured something was driving you. That first day in the library, I thought it was kind of weird that you were studying mega-farms. But the more I thought about it, the more I liked the idea. And the more I liked you.

"I thought you were exciting—not like most boys. Most boys just think about themselves—or sports. I liked the way you thought about something else.

"I'm with Carlos," she said. "I believe you about the fish. Look at that fish." She pointed to the poster.

"That fish is speaking to *me* right now. I'd like to take scuba diving lessons too. Then we could explore the oceans together. Maybe we could see that fish."

Wow! I immediately got out the phone book and wrote down the name of the dive shop. Not only will I dive again, I'll dive with Charly.

I dream about the fish all the time. Dad would probably say it's a flashback on my hallucination. In my dream, the fish speaks to me.

The seas are the bed of life. All life is interdependent. The earth is one organism Humans hold the power. Don't be shortsighted. Go slowly. Gather information. If the seas die, we all die. Tell them.

This is as far as my story goes—for now. For I've passed the message on—to you.

About the Author

M. J. Cosson loves animals of all shapes and sizes. She enjoys scuba diving and exploring ocean life.

Ms. Cosson has written many books for children, including *Sea Monsters: Myth and Truth*, *The Elephant's Ancestors*, and the Kooties Club Mystery series.